D0269035

The Twelve Dancing Princesses

Other brilliant stories to collect:

The Twelve Dancing Princesses

Retold by
Anne Fine

Illustrated by
Debi Gliori

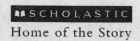
SCHOLASTIC
Home of the Story

Scholastic Children's Books,
Commonwealth House, 1–19 New Oxford Street,
London WC1A 1NU, UK
a division of Scholastic Ltd
London ~ New York ~ Toronto ~ Sydney ~ Auckland
Mexico City ~ New Delhi ~ Hong Kong

First published by Scholastic Ltd, 1998

Text copyright © Anne Fine, 1998
Illustrations © Debi Gliori, 1998

ISBN 0 590 54386 5

All rights reserved

Printed by Cox and Wyman Ltd, Reading, Berks.

2 4 6 8 10 9 7 5 3 1

The right of Anne Fine and Debi Gliori to be identified as the author
and illustrator respectively of this work has been asserted by them in
accordance with the Copyright, Designs and Patents Act, 1988.

This book is sold subject to the condition that it shall not, by way
of trade or otherwise be lent, resold, hired out, or otherwise
circulated without the publisher's prior consent in any form of
binding or cover other than that in which it is published and
without a similar condition, including this condition, being imposed
upon the subsequent purchaser.

Once upon a time, in a far away place, there lived a king who had twelve daughters. Some were pretty, and some were clever, and the youngest was as rosy as the dawn.

But was the king pleased with them? No, he was not. For each morning, as the sun rose, his daughters'

nurse tapped on his chamber door and showed him a pile of tattered shoes.

"Again, Nursie?"

"Again, Sire."

And the two of them stared forlornly at the twenty-four tattered shoes and shook their heads in amazement. For no one in the palace could understand how twelve girls could wear their freshly-stitched shoes to ribbons in a single night.

Each morning, as the sun crept over the palace wall, the king sent for his grand vizier.

"Again, Sire?"

"Again, Grand Vizier."

And the king sighed. And the nurse sighed. And the grand vizier sighed. And all of them wished that the queen was still living, so she could speak sharply to her daughters.

After his morning coffee, the king sent for Letitia. And Lottie. And Lola. And Lulu. And Louisa. And Lily. And Libby. And Lavinia. And Lena. And Laura. And Lisa. And Lara.

In they skipped. "Morning, Papa!" "Morning, Papa!" "Morning, Papa!" "Morning, Pa—"

But he was in no mood to listen to

their chirruping.

"Daughters!" he interrupted, pointing sternly to the heap of ruined shoes. "Have you been dancing?"

And the pretty ones giggled, and the clever ones were silent, and the youngest one peeped at her bare toes.

"Now, girls," scolded Nursie. "Tell your father how it is that I can shoo you into your high, high tower room, and sit outside all night and not hear a peep, and in the morning all your freshly-stitched shoes are danced to ribbons."

"Again!" scolded the grand vizier.

And still the pretty ones giggled, and the clever ones said nothing, and the youngest one peeped at her toes.

So the king sent them off with Nursie as usual, in disgrace. Then he spoke to the grand vizier.

"Easy enough to trick poor old Nursie, with her thin grey hair and her clouding eyes. Let them try tricking *you*!"

So the next night it was the grand vizier who shooed the twelve merry princesses into their high, high tower room, and sat outside the door and heard nothing.

And in the morning, all the freshly-stitched shoes were danced to ribbons.

"Right!" stormed the king. "Easy enough to fool the grand vizier with his beard down to his knees and his head full of worries. Let them try tricking *me*!"

So the next night it was the king himself who shooed his daughters, twittering like sparrows, into their high, high tower room, and sat outside all night.

And in the morning, all the freshly-stitched shoes were danced to ribbons, as usual.

Then the king lost his temper. Calling the grand vizier to his chamber, he made a proclamation and

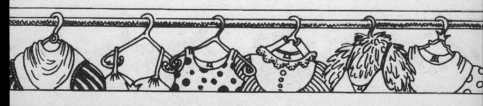

ordered him to write it down.

~

I, *the king, proclaim that*
Whosoever shall solve the mystery
of the twelve dancing princesses
(viz: where they go,
what they do,
and how their shoes are
danced to ribbons)
shall choose his favourite for a wife,
and have my kingdom, too,
when I retire or die.

~

Nursie was horrified. "But this Whosoever will see my precious girls in their nightgowns," she wailed. "And that won't do at all."

"It will be perfectly fitting," the grand vizier assured her. "Because this Whosoever will soon be the husband of one, and the brother-in-law of all the others. So he won't tell."

"But what if he *fails*?" wept Nursie. "Then this Whosoever might travel far and wide through our dominions, telling of my girls in their night-gowns."

But the king had had too little sleep

to be reasonable. Snatching the quill from the grand vizier, he scribbled at the bottom of the proclamation:

>*And Whosoever fails shall
>lose his head.*

"Happy?" snapped the king.

All the blood drained from Nursie's face. The grand vizier trembled. But before he could summon a word of wisdom or warning, the king had given the order to send the proclamation far and wide.

And far and wide the word spread. A kingdom! And a princess! Simply for staying up all night and keeping your wits about you! Young men came running: princes and paupers; butchers and candlestick makers; huntsmen and stable boys; beggars and woodcutters; minstrels and birdcatchers — everyone you could think of (except for the shoemakers, who were already doing very well). Soon there were so

many waiting outside the palace walls that the grand vizier could only give them three nights each. So every evening the staircase of the high, high tower rang with some young man's confident footsteps as he ran up to sit outside the princesses' door. And on his third and last morning, the staircase was deathly quiet as, sadly, he struggled again.

And through the taverns and market-
places of a dozen kingdoms, the same
tale was told. "I heard it all went well.
Paul (or Peter, or Percival, or Pedro)
spread his cloak outside the door of
the princesses' high, high tower room.
And Letitia (or Lottie, or Lola, or
Lulu) came in her nightgown and
handed him a goblet of the finest ruby
wine. 'Good night,' she said prettily
enough, and shut the door. And
though Paul (or Peter, or Percival, or
Pedro) heard nothing, by morning, all
twenty-four shoes had been danced to
ribbons!"

Years passed. Till one night a soldier who had fought his share of wars and was no longer young, saw something flapping from a tree in a dark wood.

It was the proclamation, torn and faded. The soldier read it through.

"Well," he said. "The hand of a princess is a fine thing to win. And I could bear with a kingdom, so long as I had a grand vizier to run it for me."

He read down to the last line.

And Whosoever fails shall
lose his head.

"Well," said the old soldier. "I have lost two of my fingers and all of my youth in the king's wars. But not my courage. Losing your head is a high price to pay for failing. But I think I shall put myself to the test."

And on he walked through the dark wood, till he caught up with an old woman dressed in black, hobbling along the path with a basket.

"Give that to me, Old Lady," said the soldier. "For even if it's filled with rocks, it will be lighter than any pack I carried in the wars."

"Wars!" grumbled the old woman. "Crops trampled! Cottages burned to ashes!" But she handed him the basket gratefully, and to be pleasant in return, asked him where he was going.

"Laugh if you will," said the soldier. "But I hope to discover the secret of the twelve dancing princesses, and win a wife and a kingdom."

The old woman looked him up and down, scars and all, and told him: "I

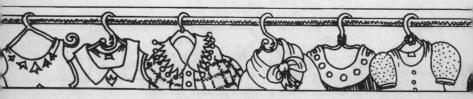

should think you would make a sensible enough king. And though I should not like to marry you if I were rosy as the dawn, for the eldest princess you will be a fine match."

Then, when they parted, she gave two things to the soldier.

First, a shabby black cloak. "It is a lot more precious than it looks," she warned. "When you put it round your shoulders, you will become invisible."

Then, some advice. "It is a lot more important than it sounds," she warned. "Don't drink the wine the princess brings to you."

So the soldier went on to the palace and told the king and the grand vizier that he wanted to try his luck. The grand vizier looked at him sadly, because it seemed to him a shame that a man should lose two fingers (not to mention his youth) in the king's wars, and then come to lose his head, too. But the rule was that anyone might try. So as the sun sank behind the palace walls, the soldier climbed

cheerfully up the steps of the high, high tower, and spread his shabby black cloak on the stone floor outside the princesses' door.

Out came the eldest (in her nightgown) to offer him a goblet of the finest ruby wine. But, remembering what the old woman in the dark wood had said, the soldier turned away towards the tower window and talked admiringly of the king's dominions as he poured the wine secretly into his beard, and down his thick fleecy jerkin, and into the plant pot at his side.

"Such lands!" he cried. "Such forests and mountains and rivers and cities!"

"Yes," said the eldest tartly. "And don't be too confident that they'll be yours."

And she shut the door firmly in his face and went back to her sisters.

The soldier stroked his grizzled beard. Well, he thought. The old woman was right. *She'll* be a match for a soldier.

Then he lay down and very quickly began to snore, as loudly as he could.

As soon as they heard him, the twelve princesses leaped out of their beds and threw off their nightgowns and opened all their chests and boxes and drawers, and lifted out their fine robes and jewels and coronets. Giggling and chattering, they helped one another into their gowns and silk stockings and freshly-stitched shoes, and each took a turn admiring herself in the looking-glass whilst the others

tripped lightly around the tower room, practising their spins and twirls and pirouettes.

But the youngest kept looking anxiously at the door.

"Something's not right," she fretted. "I feel uneasy, as if this is the night we'll be discovered."

"Silly!" scoffed the eldest, taking her hand and tugging her towards the door to peep at the snoring soldier. "How many young men have we fooled already? Too many to count. Why should this Grizzlebeard cause us any trouble? You can hear how deeply he's

sleeping already. Even without the wine, this soldier would have lost his head!"

And the soldier snored on, and shifted slightly on the shabby black cloak so that his foot went hard up against the heavy oak door, keeping it open a hair's breadth when they let go. Through the crack, he heard the footsteps turn from merry and prancing to stealthy and creeping as the eldest daughter clapped her hands and, as if by magic, her bed sank into the floor and a trapdoor opened.

Hastily, the soldier jumped to his

feet and swung the shabby black cloak around his shoulders. Silent as moonlight, he pushed open the door, and was just in time to follow the youngest as she stepped on to a secret staircase hidden in the floor, and followed her sisters down, down, down inside the palace walls.

Down past where the king was sleeping in his chamber.

Down past where the grand vizier stroked his beard and worried about high affairs of state.

Down past the kitchens and wine cellars.

Down under the earth, where the staircase was so dark that the soldier mistook his footsteps and trod on the gown of the youngest.

"Sisters!" she cried. "Something's not right! Someone has stepped on my gown."

"Silly!" "Silly!" "Silly!" "Silly!" The message passed like an echo from the eldest, through the middle sisters,

back to the youngest. "I expect you have just snagged your hem on some rusty old nail in the wall."

And none of them stopped to listen or look. So soon they stepped out at the bottom of the staircase, and the soldier found himself dazzled, for they were in a gleaming grove of silver trees.

"Can this be *real*?" he whispered to himself. "Silver trees under the earth? Or did I forget the old woman's good advice, and drink the wine?"

And, to be certain, he reached up to take a twig from the nearest tree.

Crack!

The youngest sister's hand flew to her mouth. "What was that? Oh, sisters! Did you hear?"

And the message came back from the eldest, like an echo, eleven times over. "You goose!" "You goose!" "You goose!" "It's just one of our princes, clapping for joy as he hears us approaching."

And none of them stopped to listen or look. So the soldier hurried after them, into a second grove that gleamed even more brightly than the first because the trees were all of gold.

"Gold leaves!" breathed the soldier in wonder. "Who would believe it?" And to prove that it was true, and he had seen it, he snapped off a branch.

Crack!

The youngest sister trembled. "Sisters! Surely you heard that! Something is very wrong!"

And the message came back like an echo. "You dilly!" "You dilly!" "You

dilly!" "It is only one of our princes dropping his oars in the rowlocks of his boat as we approach."

And nobody stopped. So the soldier followed them as far as a grove so bright and glittering it hurt his eyes.

"Trees of diamonds! Trees of diamonds under the earth! Sparkling brighter than frost. Glittering more brilliantly than sun on water."

The soldier's hand crept up, unbidden, and —

Crack!

A third branch was in his hand.

The youngest tore at her hair in fright. "Now, sisters, I am sure there is something wrong, and we shall be discovered!"

"You ninny!" "You ninny!" "You ninny!" The message came down the merry line from the front to the back. "That crack you heard was just the first of the fireworks our princes are sending up to greet us."

And no one stopped. So the soldier kept after them, down to a still lake where twelve little boats with twelve fine princes in them rocked on the water, waiting.

Each princess in turn stepped in with one of the princes. The soldier, thinking the boats looked more pretty than strong, thought it safest to share with the youngest. So, keeping his shabby black cloak wrapped firmly

around him, he stepped in behind her, and sat as still as stone.

And almost as heavy, it seemed. For before they were even halfway across, her young prince was grumbling. "This is a weird and wonderful thing. I'm sure I'm rowing as hard as ever I have before, yet our boat falls further and further behind the others."

The youngest princess bit her lip, and thought it was all very well to be called ninny and goose and dilly by your sisters. But a prince is different. So, though she was still uneasy, all she dared say was, "Perhaps the night's

warmer than usual," and, "Perhaps you're more tired than you think."

Soon, though, even their slow boat reached the far side of the lake, where a glorious palace, far finer than their father's, stood proudly on the shore. Its walls of pearl glowed in the moon-light, and its battlements of ivory gleamed under the stars. The most magical music poured from its case-ment windows. And there were so

many glittering guests that they spilled, laughing, out of the several ballrooms on to the terraces and into the gardens.

And how they were dancing! Every last one of them! Round and round, up and down, to and fro, here and about. As the trumpets swelled and the horns echoed, the palace and gardens rang with their laughter. First, the soldier watched from the safety of his shabby black cloak. Then the music and merriment made him bolder, and he joined in, leaping and twirling with the best of them, though still invisible. "*Fouf!*"

cried the princes as they bumped into empty air. And, "*Tish!*" cried the princesses as their goblets of wine seemed to vanish before they could drink them. But only the youngest was frightened. All the others laughed, and blamed the wine they'd drunk, and one another, and went on dancing, faster and faster, until the princes gasped for air and mercy, the princesses' coronets slipped and their shoes were in tatters, and the soldier felt as if, in one long magic night, he'd found and lived the first part of the youth he'd lost.

And then the clock struck. *Ting! Ting! Ting!*

Three o'clock! The flags were lowered and the candles snuffed, and the princesses hurried with their princes back to the lake. This time, out of pity for the youngest princess's partner, the soldier stepped in the boat of the eldest. And though they were among the first to leave the shore, by halfway over they were well behind.

"This is a strange thing," the prince could not help remarking. "I am more tired than a man should be. See how the others pull ahead."

But the eldest princess simply smiled and comforted her straining oarsman: "It always seems to me that 'well' and 'quickly' seldom meet, and I am quite happy lying here."

Yes, thought the soldier. She will make a fine match for a man with a grizzled beard like me.

As the boat reached the shore, the soldier leaped into the shallows and ran to overtake all the others. Some he passed in the first grove, some in the second, and some in the third. But by the time he reached the bottom of the staircase, he was ahead of all of them. Up, up, up, he ran. And by the time the twelve tired princesses reached their room, his glittering branches were safely hidden under his shabby

black cloak, and he was snoring in earnest.

"See?" said the eldest. "Here's your old soldier, dreaming. Where are your worries now?" And she pulled the youngest sister's dress over her head for her, and hung it on a hook, and tucked her sleepy sister into bed, and threw her tattered shoes into the pile in the corner.

In the morning, the soldier woke and said to himself, "These things I've seen are such great marvels that I will take my full three days to see them again."

So all day he said nothing to the king or the grand vizier. And the next night, and the next, he followed the princesses down the dark staircase and through the glittering groves, and over the lake to the palace.

And there, like them, he danced till three o'clock — except that, in the strange magic of being invisible, he did not, like them, wear out his shoes.

And when he was tired with dancing, he stole wine from one or another of the princesses' gold cups, and leaned back in some empty chair, and drank a toast to the old woman in the dark wood, and listened to the fine music. On the second night, he told himself: "Now I have had the second part of my lost youth." And on the third: "Now I have had it all, and will grow old content." So, to remind himself of the splendour and ease and glory of these three special nights, as they left for the last time he took with him a golden cup he had stolen from under

the eldest princess's hand when she stood up to dance.

On that third and last morning, the grand vizier rose with an even heavier heart than usual. He had enjoyed the company of the soldier, and didn't want to see him lose his head. So he dillied and dallied, until the king clapped his hands and ordered,

"Fetch in the man who claims he

can tell me where my daughters go at night, and what they do."

The twelve princesses crept along the passage in their bare feet to listen to what this snoring fool would say. How pale their faces looked when the soldier unwrapped his shabby black cloak and out fell branches of silver and gold and diamonds, and a golden cup.

At the sight of these marvels, the grand vizier trembled with hope, and Nursie's heart lifted at the thought that she might never again have to hear the sad shuffle of footsteps down

the tower stairs. Then the soldier stood fearlessly and told all who were listening where he had been and what he had seen. Each time he saw disbelief rising in their eyes, he pointed to the glittering branches and the golden cup.

The king was silent. Then he said, "I will hear what my daughters have to say," and sent Nursie to fetch them.

In they all trooped, the pretty ones giggling, the clever ones silent, and the youngest one peeping at her toes.

The king said to the eldest, "Is it true what this soldier says about a magical palace under the earth, and lakes and princes and dancing?"

The eldest looked reproachfully at the soldier. But he looked firmly back at her. And some of the courage he'd brought back from her father's wars was in her own heart, too, because she stood fearlessly and told all who were listening,

"Yes. It is true."

Then the king ordered the grand vizier to fetch the proclamation and told the soldier he must choose one of the twelve princesses for his wife.

Everyone's eyes crept to the youngest, for she was as rosy as the dawn. But the soldier remembered what the old woman had told him, and said cheerfully and wisely:

"I am no longer young, so I will choose the eldest. I am sure she and I will make a fine match."

So they did, too. And when the old king died, the soldier took his place, and made an excellent ruler with the help of the grand vizier. He was kind to his sisters-in-law and built them a ballroom — nowhere near as fine as the other, but still excellent for dancing.

And the grand vizier grew his beard on down to his feet.

And Nursie sat knitting peaceably for Samuel. And Sapphire. And Silas. And Serena. And Sidney. And Salome. And Septimus. And Sukie. And Stanley. And Sabrina. And Simon. And Baby Sappho, who kept peeping

at her toes.

And the new king ordered the grand vizier to be sure there were no more wars in the old woman's corner of the kingdom. Or anywhere else, for that matter. So there were no more burnt cottages, no more trampled crops. And every week, like clockwork, a basket was sent to her, filled to the brim with bread and eggs and meat and wine. So she was contented, too, in her dark wood, and thought it a very fine bargain for a shabby black cloak and a piece of advice, even if both were magic.

And everyone – everyone – danced every night of the week.

And they were all happy ever after.

Other stories to collect:

Aesop's Fables

Malorie Blackman
Illustrated by Patrice Aggs

Once upon a time there was a man named Aesop
who told stories full of wisdom...

Hansel and Gretel

Henrietta Branford
Illustrated by Lesley Harker

Once upon a time there were a brother and sister
who were left alone in the forest...

The Snow Queen

Berlie Doherty
Illustrated by Siân Bailey

Once upon a time there was a little boy whose
heart was turned to ice...

The Goose Girl

Gillian Cross
Illustrated by Jason Cockcroft

Once upon a time there was a princess who lost
everything she ever owned...

Grey Wolf, Prince Jack and the Firebird

Alan Garner

Illustrated by James Mayhew

Once upon a time there was a prince who set out
to seek the mysterious firebird...

Mossycoat

Philip Pullman

Illustrated by Peter Bailey

Once upon a time there was a beautiful girl whose
mother made her a magical, mossy coat...

The Six Swan Brothers

Adèle Geras
Illustrated by Ian Beck

Once upon a time there was a brave princess
who saw her six brothers turned into swans...

The Seal Hunter

Tony Mitton
Illustrated by Nick Maland

Once upon a time there was a cruel fisherman
who was dragged to the bottom of the ocean
by a seal prince...

Cockadoodle-doo, Mr Sultana!

Michael Morpurgo
Illustrated by Michael Foreman

Once upon a time there was a rich and greedy
sultan who met a clever little cockerel...

Rapunzel

Jacqueline Wilson
Illustrated by Nick Sharratt

Once upon a time there a baby who was stolen
by a witch...

Rumpelstiltskin

Kit Wright
Illustrated by Ted Dewan

Once upon a time there was a beautiful girl who
would die if she couldn't spin straw into gold...

The Three Heads
in the Well

Susan Gates
Illustrated by Sue Heap

Once upon a time there were two stepsisters who
went out to seek their fortunes...